W9-ANP-907

THE NAUGHTIEST GIRL
SAVES THE DAY

The Further Adventures of Enid Blyton's
Naughtiest Girl

The Naughtiest Girl Saves The Day

Anne Digby

Hodder
Children's
Books

a division of Hodder Headline Limited

Copyright © 1999 The Enid Blyton Company
Enid Blyton's signature is a Registered Trade Mark of
Enid Blyton Ltd.
All rights reserved

First published in Great Britain in 1999
by Hodder Children's Books
This edition published in 2005
For sale in the Indian Sub-continent only

10

The right of Enid Blyton to be identified as the Author of
the Work has been asserted by her in accordance with
the Copyright, Designs and Patents Act 1988.

For further information on Enid Blyton,
please contact www.blyton.com

All rights reserved. Apart from any use permitted under
UK copyright law, this publication may only be reproduced,
stored or transmitted, in any form, or by any means with prior
permission in writing of the publishers or in the case of
reprographic production in accordance with the terms of licences
issued by the Copyright Licensing Agency and may not be
otherwise circulated in any form of binding or cover other than that
in which it is published and without a similar condition being
imposed on the subsequent purchaser.

All characters in this publication are fictitious and any resemblance
to real persons, living or dead, is purely coincidental.

A Catalogue record for this book is available from
the British Library

ISBN 0 340 91099 2

Typeset by Avon Dataset Ltd, Bidford-on-Avon, Warks

Printed and bound in India by
Gopsons Papers Ltd., Noida

Hodder Children's Books
a division of Hodder Headline Limited
338 Euston Road
London NW1 3BH

Contents

1 Elizabeth and Julian are together again

'Perhaps the train from London's running late!' said Elizabeth impatiently. 'Do you think so, Joan? Or perhaps the coach from the station has broken down! Do you think it could be stuck halfway up the hill with a flat tyre? Just imagine all the boys and girls having to sit inside the stuffy hot coach waiting for the wheel to be changed . . .'

Elizabeth jigged from one foot to the other, restlessly. She was at the top of the stone steps, outside the main doors of Whyteleafe School. Her gaze kept darting to the big stone archway through which the school coach was due to appear.

'. . . what do *you* think, Joan?' she finished.

Joan was Elizabeth's best friend at Whyteleafe School, although slightly older and in the second form. She was as calm and sensible as Elizabeth was excitable and impulsive. She shook her head and smiled at her friend.

'*I* think you have a vivid imagination, Elizabeth. That's what *I* think!' she said quietly. 'The coach is hardly late at all yet.'

'But it was due at half-past one and that was five minutes ago!' protested Elizabeth. 'And I'm starving hungry, aren't you, Joan? And none of us can go into the dining hall and have dinner until everyone's back from half term!'

It was true that Elizabeth was hungry and regretted the fact that dinner would be late today. The delicious smell of savoury pies baking in the big ovens had wafted over to her from the kitchens. And, much earlier, she had seen the domestic staff preparing heaps of new potatoes and carrots from the school gardens. They would no doubt be steaming merrily away by now. There was always an especially good meal after a holiday, when many boys and girls were hungry at the end of a long journey back to their boarding school.

But there was more to it than that.

'As a matter of fact, I'm really looking forward to seeing my class again, Joan,' she confessed. 'Especially Julian. I'm longing to tell him about the notice that Miss Ranger has put up on the notice-board. It's going to make our English lessons really exciting!'

Most of the first form had gone home for the half term holiday, including Elizabeth's special friend, Julian. Elizabeth had stayed on at school for a summer camp in the grounds. There had been lots of ups and downs but all in all it had been a wonderful adventure. Now she was looking forward to the second half of the summer term, sleeping in a proper bed again and life getting back to normal.

'Hello, Daniel! You're one of the last back!' she called out cheerfully, as an open-topped car cruised by. Daniel Carter was one of her classmates and only lived in the next village. As with any child who lived near Whyteleafe, he was being brought back to school by car. 'You should have been one of the first!'

The pale, fair-haired boy was sitting in the back of the open car, reading a book. He looked up briefly and returned Elizabeth's wave, then immediately turned his attention back to his book.

'Have you seen the coach?' she shouted. But the car had passed them now and her words were carried away on the breeze.

'It must be such fun to ride in an open car like that,' commented Joan. 'What an unusual boy Daniel is, nose stuck in a book as his father drives him along!'

'Yes, he does seem to prefer his books to the sights and sounds of the real world and to having friends,' agreed Elizabeth. 'I think shyness has a lot to do with it.'

'But he's a great one for complaining about people at School Meetings,' Joan pointed out. 'That's not the best way to make friends.'

'Yes, wasn't it funny that time he grumbled about Arabella making faces at him?' laughed Elizabeth. 'He makes himself sound such a baby when he stands up with silly Grumbles and Complaints. It's such a shame he can't learn to be a good mixer because then people would like him more.'

'I expect Whyteleafe will lick him into shape in time,' smiled Joan. 'You know that better than anyone, Elizabeth. When you first came here, you were the Naughtiest Girl in the School!'

'Yes. I've been trying to live it down ever since!' groaned Elizabeth. Her Naughtiest Girl nickname had stuck and no doubt always would! 'Oh, Joan, wasn't I horrid?' she sighed.

She stared across the green lawns to the trees beyond. A bird wheeled above them in the cloudless blue sky. It was so lovely at Whyteleafe, thought Elizabeth.

'I did everything I could think of to get myself sent home, didn't I?' she continued. 'From the best school in the whole world!'

'I'm so glad you didn't succeed,' said Joan quietly, giving her friend's hand a squeeze. 'I really am.'

A few moments later a large coach with WHYTELEAFE SCHOOL on the front came nosing through the archway.

'It's here!' whooped Elizabeth. 'Hurray! Now *everybody's* back!'

The coach pulled up at the foot of the steps. All the boys and girls who had been on the London train came tumbling out. Elizabeth ran down to greet them. Joan, as befitted a second form monitor, followed at a more dignified pace to meet some of her own classmates.

'Julian!' squealed Elizabeth, her brown curls bouncing.

'Hello, Naughtiest Girl!' grinned the dark haired boy, his cousin, Patrick, just behind him. 'How was camp then?'

'It was wonderful! But listen, Julian, such an exciting notice has gone up on the board. Wait till you see it! Miss Ranger's just put it up this morning. It's our form's turn to put on the Summer Play this year! It will be performed outside, in the school grounds! If we want to try for a part, we've got to sign up on the notice. The auditions are going to take place during English lessons!' Elizabeth had been bottling this news up for over an hour and it was now pouring out like a torrent. 'Oh, Julian, wouldn't it be fun if you and I could get the lead parts? The play's called *A Woodland Adventure* and it's been written by the joint heads!'

She tugged at Julian's hand.

'Come on, let's run. If we hurry, we'll be the first to get our names on the list—'

'Hey, steady on, Miss Whirlwind—' began Julian, looking amused.

'Yes, steady on, Elizabeth,' smiled Miss Thomas, as she shepherded the last of the children off the coach. She could see that the Naughtiest Girl was trying to whisk Julian away! 'Julian's not allowed to disappear off anywhere at the moment. Everyone from the London train's been given strict instructions to go straight to the dining hall, as soon as they've washed their hands and faces. I suggest you do the same, Elizabeth. We're all very hungry. Whatever it is, it will have to wait.'

Elizabeth sighed and knew that she would have to be patient.

2 Elizabeth's hopes are kept alive

Julian refused to hurry through dinner. He was very hungry and wanted second helpings of everything. Elizabeth had to agree that the savoury pie was one of the tastiest that Cook had ever baked. The new potatoes and carrots were mouthwatering. And pudding was treacle tart and custard, one of their favourites.

It was a very jolly meal, with everyone catching up on everyone else's news. Some of the children had been to see shows in London. Ruth and Tessa had been taken to Regents Park Zoo by Tessa's mother. Patrick had been at Lords all week with his father, watching the cricket. Patrick was slightly boring on the subject but Elizabeth didn't mind at all, feeling happy to be surrounded by her classmates once again. Julian claimed that he had done absolutely nothing apart from laze around and go swimming once or twice.

Elizabeth, Belinda and Kathleen enjoyed telling the others about school camp. Arabella, who had behaved badly at camp and got into trouble, was suitably subdued.

'What's the matter, Arabella? Didn't you enjoy camping out very much?' asked Julian lightly. He was always very quick and shrewd. 'You don't seem to be saying very much about it.'

The spoilt girl screwed up her dainty, doll-like face and gave a little shrug.

'It was all right,' she murmured.

Elizabeth had no intention of telling tales on Arabella but she felt a quiet satisfaction. Arabella not saying much made a very pleasant change!

However, this happy state of affairs didn't last long.

At the end of the meal, the conversation turned to the exciting news about the first form play. Kathleen, like Elizabeth, had seen the notice that Miss Ranger, their form teacher, had placed on the notice-board and she had been spreading the news.

'Let's all go and put our names down for it!' she said. 'Oh, won't it be fun, doing the auditions in English lessons.'

'I've put my name down already,' announced Arabella. 'And I've read the play! As soon as Miss Ranger put the notice up, I asked to borrow a copy. It's absolutely brilliant.'

'It's all about a little girl called Fay who falls asleep in the woods!' interrupted Arabella's friend, Rosemary. She was very excited. 'When Fay wakes up, she's turned into a beautiful fairy queen and she has all these wonderful adventures with a goblin called Jonkin and they meet all these woodland creatures . . .'

'Miss Belle and Miss Best wrote the play themselves,' said Arabella, knowledgeably. 'They wrote it especially for us. Apparently it's five years since the first form had a turn of performing the Summer Play and they want it to be really special. Oh, aren't the joint heads clever to have written a whole new play?'

'And the part of Fay is just *made* for Arabella!' gabbled Rosemary. 'Can't you just see her as a fairy queen? I can. Of course,' she added, quickly, 'there will be lots of other parts for everyone and lots of things to do, like make costumes and things. I'm hoping to be chosen as prompter,' she added modestly.

Elizabeth listened to all this in stunned silence.

Arabella and Rosemary were now getting up from the table, keen to be off. Rosemary was still gabbling in excitement.

'Shall we go and get the play from your desk, Arabella? We'll take it outside as you suggested! I'm longing to hear you read bits out loud. It will be good practice for you! I wonder which boy will be chosen to play Jonkin? Oh, that's going to be a good part, too, isn't it—'

Arabella turned back and gave Julian a dazzling smile.

'I think Julian would make a wonderful Jonkin!' she simpered. 'Jonkin wears a mask in the play but he has green eyes, just like Julian, and he's very funny and clever. I do hope you'll put your name down, Julian!'

As the two girls left the dining hall, Elizabeth bent her head over the last of her treacle tart, struggling to keep calm. In a blur she heard some of the others chattering as they started to drift away from the table . . .

'My goodness! Arabella's staked her claim quickly, hasn't she?'

'Trust her!'

'You have to admit she *might* make a good fairy queen. She'd look the part, at least, with that dainty little face of hers.'

'Too doll-like. Not vivacious enough.'

'Well, let's go and have a look at this notice.'

'Might as well put our names down. It's going to be fun.'

Before long, only Elizabeth, Julian and Patrick were left sitting at the long table, all on their own.

'I *knew* we should have rushed and put our names on the list, Julian!' she said crossly, trying hard not to scowl. Arabella had got her name down first. Probably right at the head of the list! Not only that, she'd got hold of a copy of the play already. She'd read it through and was about to start practising for the auditions. 'Now Arabella's got a head start on everybody else!'

'Well, blowed if I would want to play the part

of a fairy queen!' said Julian. He was laughing at her. 'And if *you* want to, Elizabeth, you'd better stop scowling and looking like a bold, bad girl and practise looking pretty!'

'I don't know *what* I want now,' said Elizabeth sulkily. 'Perhaps Arabella *would* be best. Perhaps I wouldn't be any good. And besides, she's got her name at the top of the list now.'

'You silly bumpkin.' Julian tweaked her hair. 'As if that makes the slightest difference to anything! Miss Ranger will just give out the parts to whoever reads them best when the auditions take place. I should think Arabella would be much too wooden. Now, you just run along, and sign up as you said you were going to.'

Elizabeth immediately felt cheerful again.

'I will, too!' she exclaimed, smiling and clapping her hands. 'But—'

She looked at Julian anxiously.

'—what about you, Julian? Surely you want to be in the play, too? It won't be half as much fun if you're not in it. Arabella's probably right about you being the goblin. I can just imagine you!'

Julian yawned.

'I don't think acting's quite my line, Elizabeth,' he said gently.

Patrick, sitting further along the table and toying with the last of his treacle tart, suddenly looked up when Julian said that.

Elizabeth was about to start arguing with Julian. She knew perfectly well that her friend was a natural actor, brilliant at voices and imitations and altogether very funny. What he really meant was that the idea of being in the first form play bored him. How typical. How mean of him!

But before she could open her mouth to protest, Patrick spoke for the first time. He had been looking rather gloomy but now he had suddenly perked up. He couldn't help being a little jealous of his cousin, who was so full of talent, so good at everything he touched. To hear Julian being praised, even by Arabella, had made him smart.

'Glad to hear you've got some sense in your

head after all, Julian,' he said. 'Wouldn't like to see my dear cousin make a complete fool of himself.'

'Oh, so that's what you think, is it?' asked Julian sharply.

He suddenly got to his feet.

'Come on, Elizabeth. Let's go along and sign up for this play then.'

Patrick watched them go, open-mouthed.

'I thought you didn't want to be in it!' he said crossly.

Julian glanced back over his shoulder.

'I've changed my mind,' he said, carelessly. 'It should be fun. A chance to make a complete fool of myself!'

As the two of them left the dining hall and headed towards the school notice-board, Elizabeth felt rather sorry for Julian's cousin. She might have guessed that, whatever Patrick wanted, Julian would want to do the exact opposite.

As they wrote their names up on the list, she felt hopeful all over again. It would be wonderful to be chosen for the lead part and to play opposite Julian. He would make everything such fun.

Who else had signed up?

She looked at the names. There were slightly more girls than boys so far. But there was one name that was rather unexpected.

'Look, Julian!' she exclaimed. 'Daniel Carter's signed up.'

All through dinner he had, as usual, sat furtively reading a book under the table and not taken the slightest interest in the conversation about the play. Daniel never joined in any activities that he could possibly avoid.

'What a surprise,' said Julian. 'Do you think he's hoping for the main boy's part, the goblin?'

Elizabeth laughed happily.

'With you around, Julian,' she replied, 'I'm afraid he'll just have to hope away!'

3 Daniel drops a mysterious hint

In the English lesson the next day, Daniel hardly looked like somebody hoping to land a good part in the play. He looked rather glum about the whole thing!

'Here's yours, Daniel,' said Miss Ranger, brightly, as she finished handing out copies of the play to those who had signed up. 'When you read it, you will find it's a very good play. I want you to study it carefully over the next few days and decide which part to try for. You must learn some lines from your favourite part. And –' the teacher looked up and smiled round at the class '– the same thing applies to the rest of you. Please try to learn some of the lines you wish to speak when we have the auditions next week. You'll be able to act a part so much better if you do not have to read it from the script.'

'I've learnt some of my lines already!' piped up Arabella, smugly.

'Are you sure?' asked the teacher, kindly. She knew how much difficulty the oldest girl in the form had with memorising things.

Elizabeth was pleased that the auditions were still a few days away. They would be held during English lessons next week and the joint heads would be sitting in on some of the judging! Arabella had tried to steal a march but now they all had a chance to catch up. It was very pleasing.

Daniel, however, did not look in the least bit pleased. Elizabeth, sitting on the corner of Julian's desk and eagerly leafing through the play, had noticed how reluctantly the fair-haired boy had collected his copy, the last member of the class to do so. Now he walked back to his desk, opened the lid, and placed it inside without even glancing at it. Then he sat down and folded his arms.

As Miss Ranger addressed the class, he looked glummer than ever. She was telling them how, later on, rehearsals for the play would have to take place out of school hours – and in the fresh air. As the Summer Play was always held out of doors, it would be good practice for the children to get used to acting outside!

Daniel hated any form of outdoor activity. He was one of the few children at Whyteleafe to have his own tiny room, up on the attic floor above the main dormitories. Summer or winter, he loved his cosy little room under the eaves, where he could read his favourite story books to his heart's content.

'So be prepared to give up some spare time, those of you who are chosen,' concluded the teacher. 'We have so much other work to get through in English lessons. Remember, you have exams at the end of term and very important ones, too, for those who wish to go up to the second form in September. So now,' she clapped her hands briskly, 'stop talking everyone, please, and return to your desks and get out your spelling books.'

But by now Elizabeth was chattering away non-stop to Julian.

'Doesn't the story look fun, Julian? I *can* just

see you as Jonkin! I don't in the least mind giving up my spare time if I'm chosen, do you? I'll have to skip some of my piano practice! But have you noticed something?' She lowered her voice to a whisper. 'Have you noticed how grumpy Daniel looks about the whole thing? I can't imagine anyone who would hate acting more, especially out of doors! So why did he put his name down?'

'I think there's probably a very simple answer,' Julian whispered back. He, too, had noted carefully Daniel's attitude. 'I don't think the poor boy wants to be in the play, at all. I think one of the teachers *ordered* him to put his name down for it. Perhaps Miss Ranger herself. It must worry them a bit, the way he never joins in anything.'

'Oh, Julian! You are clever!' responded Elizabeth. 'Yes, that must be the answer—'

'ELIZABETH!' exclaimed Miss Ranger. 'Please stop talking and get off Julian's desk. Julian, please get your spelling book out as you have been asked to do. I think I will have to separate you two.'

The teacher looked around the room and then

pointed to an empty desk, all on its own, at the back of the classroom under the open window.

'Elizabeth, please get your books and move to that desk at the back. You love talking so much that I think it will be better for you.' She spoke to the little girl quite kindly. 'You will be out of temptation's way there and I know I can trust you to pay attention and work hard, even right at the back there.'

'Yes, Miss Ranger,' replied Elizabeth.

Julian looked at his friend apologetically but Elizabeth did not mind in the least. She knew that Miss Ranger was acting for the best and besides, it was a lovely place, there by the open window. There were soft summer scents wafting in on the warm breeze. The last thing Elizabeth wanted to do at present was to blot her copybook by talking to her friends in class. Now any temptation to do so had been removed.

She pondered upon what Julian had said. *Poor Daniel*! she thought.

But the very same day, at the end of the afternoon, Daniel caused them another surprise.

*   *   *

Once lessons were finished for the day, Elizabeth and Julian went for a short ride in the grounds on the ponies. Emerging from the trees afterwards, they dismounted and walked the horses back to the school stables. A boy was leaning against one of the stable doors, as though enjoying the sunshine. He waved cheerfully when he saw them and hurried forward to greet them.

'Hello, Julian! Hello, Elizabeth!' he exclaimed, whilst patting the horses' necks. 'Isn't it a lovely day! Have you had a good ride?'

It was Daniel.

The two friends unsaddled their horses and rubbed them down, at the same time glancing at each other in astonishment. It was such a surprise to see Daniel out in the fresh air! He looked so happy, too. His cheeks were flushed and there was an air of suppressed excitement about him. What could have happened to bring about such a change in him? It was most perplexing.

'Isn't it a grand day?' he repeated, once the ponies were unsaddled. 'Here, I'll put the tack away for you and shut the ponies up for the stableman.'

'Will you really?' said Julian, gratefully.

'That's sweet of you, Daniel,' said Elizabeth. They dumped the tack and were about to leave when—

'Do you two know when the next School Meeting is?' the boy blurted out eagerly.

'Friday,' replied Elizabeth. 'Why?'

'Planning a Complaint, Daniel?' asked Julian, teasingly. 'Or possibly a Grumble?'

The boy flushed.

'No, not at all. Nobody's done anything to annoy me at present,' he said solemnly. 'I've got a special request to make to the Meeting, that's all. A *very* special request!'

'Whatever's that?' asked Elizabeth, fascinated.

'I – I'm sorry, I can't tell you. Not yet . . .'

'Oh, please do!' begged Elizabeth. 'Why can't you tell us?'

'I – I've got to see how things go,' mumbled the boy. 'I'm sorry. I shouldn't have said anything. I didn't mean to intrigue you . . .'

He looked apologetic.

'Fair enough,' said Julian, turning to walk away.

Daniel hurried forward and grabbed Julian's arm.

'But please, if I do ... when I do ask the Meeting this thing, I do hope you two will support me. Please.'

Elizabeth was more intrigued than ever.

'I'm sure we will if we can, Daniel.'

'Once we know what it is!' laughed Julian.

It was such a surprising episode. The two friends talked about it all the way back to the school building. Daniel had seemed so very different from his usual self.

'Whatever's happened to him?' wondered Julian. 'Can that be the same chap who looked so glum in English this morning?'

An anxious thought suddenly crossed Elizabeth's mind.

'You don't think it's because he's read the play by now? And he's realised what a brilliant play it is and how brilliant the part of Jonkin is, and how this is his big chance to shine ... ?'

She hated the idea of anyone other than Julian having the part.

'Hardly! He'd be up in that little room of his, learning it off by heart, not enjoying himself in the fresh air for a change,' replied Julian. 'No, I'm sure it's not that. But something's transformed him, all right.'

'Can it be to do with this mysterious request he wants to put to the School Meeting?' pondered Elizabeth. 'I can't think what it's going to be.'

'We'll find out,' said Julian, airily, 'soon enough.'

4 An interesting School Meeting

On Friday, lessons over for the week, Elizabeth ran up to the dormitory and got ready for the School Meeting. She washed her hands and brushed her hair and decided that today she would wear her school blazer, even though it was still a bit big for her. As she did up the shiny silver buttons and looked in the mirror, she felt a happy, belonging sort of feeling.

She was proud to wear the blazer and to be a member of Whyteleafe School. She admired the way that William and Rita, the head-boy and head-girl, ran the Meetings with the pupils themselves making all kinds of important decisions about any problems that arose, without any help from the teachers.

As she filed into the hall with Belinda, Kathleen and Jenny she looked at her watch.

They were early. But somebody else had got there ahead of them.

Daniel, usually one of the last, was seated very near the front at the far end of an empty bench. The girls took their places alongside him and Elizabeth noticed how spruce he looked. He was sitting upright, arms folded, waiting for the Meeting to begin. He seemed very alert. There was still the same air of suppressed excitement about him that had been there for some days.

Others, as well as Elizabeth and Julian, had noticed the change in Daniel. Although he still took a book with him everywhere, he was spending much more time out of doors. He looked happier and more lively. He had even begun to take an interest in the Summer Play. Apparently he'd learned bits from several different parts and had shyly asked Martin to test him.

Well, now we shall find out more, at last, thought Elizabeth. *He looks quite keyed up about this special request of his, whatever it is!*

The twelve school monitors came and took

their places on the platform behind William and Rita, who were seated at a special table. There was a big book on the table. Important things that happened at Meetings were always written down in the Book. The scene never failed to remind Elizabeth of a court room, with William and Rita as the judges and the monitors, the jury.

The hall soon filled up as all the classes came in. Miss Belle and Miss Best, the joint heads, and Mr Johns, the senior master, slipped quietly into their special chairs, right at the back. They were there to observe proceedings but never joined in unless their advice was requested.

When everybody was seated and the hubbub of chatter was reaching a crescendo, William picked up a small hammer and struck the table loudly.

'Silence, please! The Meeting will now begin.'

As the gavel went down Elizabeth, as always, felt a frisson of excitement. There was an instant hush all around her. What would today's Meeting bring?

'First of all, finance,' said William. 'A lot of

you will have brought money back with you. Thomas is passing the School Box along the rows. Please place all your money inside.'

There came the rustle of bank notes and the merry rattle of coins going into the big box as the children cheerfully parted with their money. Some of the campers had been sent postal orders. They went into the box, too. It was a strict rule at Whyteleafe that all spending money was pooled and then shared out fairly, so that no pupil had an unfair advantage over another.

After that, every child in the school was handed two pounds. This was their spending money for the week.

'Now, are there any requests for extra money?' asked the head-girl.

Eileen put her hand up.

'Please, Rita, I broke a string in my racket at team practice yesterday. We've got a match soon but Mr Warlow has had a look at it and he feels the racket's so worn that I really need to have a new one and just keep the old one as a spare.'

Rita had a quick word with William and they both nodded.

'That tennis racket of yours has had a lot of wear and tear this term in the service of the school, Eileen,' smiled Rita. 'No wonder it's worn out. You will be allocated some money to buy a new one.'

Patrick, who was in the second tennis team with Eileen, looked pleased for her sake. Now she would play even better.

The next request was rather more difficult to deal with.

A member of the junior class (which always sat cross-legged on the floor in the front of the first form benches) rose to his feet.

'Please, I'm getting very keen on tennis now we're starting to learn but I haven't got my own racket. There's one in the school second-hand shop and it only costs five pounds. Could I have some extra money to help me buy it?'

The head-boy and girl went into a huddle with the monitors to discuss the request. After two or three minutes, they returned to the table and William called for silence.

'We don't think we can donate you any money from the pool, Henry, because it wouldn't be fair on any other juniors who don't own a racket. What we are prepared to do is to advance you your next two weeks' pocket money. With today's money that would mean you have six pounds.'

The little boy looked very disappointed.

'But then, please William, that would only leave me a pound for sweets and things to last me three whole weeks!'

'Yes, Henry,' said Rita kindly. 'So this offer is a good test for you. It will help you to decide just *how* keen you are on tennis and how much you want your own racket, rather than using the school ones while you're learning. Think about it for a while. Then let us know at the end of the Meeting what you have decided.'

'Yes, Rita.'

'Any more requests for money, anybody?' she asked.

Elizabeth glanced sidelong at Daniel. But he remained silent.

So whatever he intended to ask for, then, did

not require spending money.

The Meeting moved briskly on to discuss the school camp. William proposed a vote of thanks for the tent monitors, explaining that they had all done an excellent job. Sitting on the platform, Joan looked proud and gave Elizabeth a grateful wave. Only they knew about the problems she had had as a tent monitor and how they had been overcome.

After that came Grumbles or Complaints.

There were none at all this week.

'Good,' said William. 'We have just one more important matter to deal with. After that we will finish up with Any Other Business . . .'

'Nearly there, Daniel,' whispered Elizabeth behind her hand, smiling. 'You'll soon be able to ask what you want to ask.'

'I know!' nodded Daniel, looking eager and excited.

Elizabeth suddenly noticed how solemn William was looking.

'I'm sorry to have to tell you,' William was saying, 'that the matter we now have to deal with is a serious one. John, would you please stand up and tell the Meeting what you have told Rita and me?'

John Terry, the head-boy of the school garden and one of Elizabeth's favourite people, rose to his feet. He was a blunt, straightforward boy who had great gifts as a gardener but none for public speaking.

'Some little idiot's been vandalising the strawberry beds!' he blurted out, dark spots of anger on his cheeks. 'Somebody too greedy to wait for the fruit to get ripe! Pulling up the plants to see if any of the underneath berries are red yet, I daresay. Uprooting the plants with all the berries still green!'

There were shocked gasps around the hall. Whispers rippled up and down the rows of children. What a mean thing to do. Another month of ripening sun and the school gardens always produced big, luscious red strawberries – heaps of them. Strawberries and cream for tea ... They all loved strawberry time! But any plants pulled up by the roots would die now before the fruit could ripen properly.

'How greedy and silly!' whispered Elizabeth.

'Greedy and silly and ignorant,' agreed Kathleen.

William banged the gavel for silence. There was more drama to come. He held something up between his thumb and forefinger. Everybody looked at it.

It was a shiny, silver blazer button.

'Here is something very interesting,' he said. 'The person concerned lost their blazer button while they were hunting for strawberries. John found this lying amongst the uprooted plants. Would the person responsible now own up,' he said, with heavy irony, 'and we can give them their blazer button back.'

There was silence.

'Stand up and own up, please,' repeated William.

They all held their breath and waited. A half minute ticked by. But still nobody moved.

'Very well,' said William, at last. 'Whoever behaved in this stupid way will no doubt have friends and classmates. *They* will notice that someone has a blazer button missing. Will they please persuade the person concerned to come to our study and own up? John has a great number of jobs in the garden waiting for them. Now, is there any other business, please, before we close the Meeting?'

In the drama of what had just taken place, Elizabeth had forgotten all about Daniel's special request. But she glanced at him now. He, too, seemed to have forgotten it! He was just sitting there, staring into space.

'Come on, Daniel!' she whispered, giving him a nudge.

The boy gave a start. Then, slowly, he put his hand up.

'Yes, Daniel?' asked Rita.

'I – I –' The fair-haired boy got to his feet, looking very self-conscious. Now that his big moment had come, he seemed embarrassed and tongue-tied. Poor Daniel! Elizabeth felt sorry for him. It was obviously something very important to him. It was daunting to have to ask in front of the whole school like this.

'Go on!' she encouraged.

'Please, can I help with the horses and muck out the stables and things?' he blurted out. 'I know Robert helps sometimes and I'd like to as well.'

Rita looked at Daniel in surprise. This was hardly something that needed to be brought to a School Meeting.

'Well, only the stableman can decide that, Daniel,' she said, gently. 'I'm sure he'll be pleased to have some extra help and can find you some jobs to do. You must go and talk to him about it.'

Daniel sat down. His face was bright red.

Elizabeth stared at him in amazement. He had never taken the slightest interest in the school stables before. He was one of the few children in the class who never rode. But, above all, she felt cheated somehow. A sense of disappointment. Whatever had Daniel been making such a fuss about?

'What a let down!' she said to Julian, after the Meeting. 'What was so special about that? Why did he beg us to support him, the other day? What a fuss about nothing! Oh, Julian, I do think Daniel is peculiar!'

'He's certainly a puzzle,' said Julian, with

a shrug. 'But I'm more interested in this strawberry mystery.'

5 The auditions take place

'The mystery of who pulled up the strawberry plants? You're right Julian,' nodded Elizabeth. 'That *is* rather interesting!'

It was annoying of Daniel to have been so tantalising about something so tame. But now the Meeting had given them something different to think about! Poor John. What a shock it must have been to find some of his plants uprooted. She fully intended to spend some time in the school gardens this weekend and ask for some jobs to do. Could any of the plants be rescued?

'What puzzles me is why they didn't own up,' said Julian. 'People usually do.'

'Too scared, I suppose!' sighed Elizabeth. 'Too scared and cowardly.'

'But they must know they're going to be found out,' reasoned Julian, digging his hands deep in his pockets. He looked at the three gleaming silver buttons on Elizabeth's blazer. 'Our school blazers only have three buttons on them. If you've lost one of them, you can't exactly hide the fact!'

'Yes,' agreed Elizabeth. 'And wasn't it funny to be wearing a blazer in the first place? I know I wouldn't wear mine if I were just messing about in the school gardens.'

'That's exactly what I was thinking,' replied Julian.

'But it's lucky they were!' said Elizabeth, cheerfully. 'That blazer button is a wonderful clue. It's bound to catch them out before long. We could do some detective work ourselves, Julian. We'll start looking at everybody who's wearing a blazer.'

'Quite wrong, Elizabeth!' replied Julian.

'Wrong, why?' asked Elizabeth, indignantly.

Julian looked amused.

'We must start looking at everybody who *isn't* wearing a blazer. There will be somebody, somewhere, who never wants to wear their blazer for some reason!'

'Because they're too scared?' realised Elizabeth. 'Oh, of course.'

'Yes. And that's going to be much more difficult. An interesting challenge.'

They both agreed to keep their eyes open. They were not the only ones.

The mystery of the vandalised strawberry plants was a major talking point as they went into tea that day. Everybody wearing a blazer was subjected to scrutiny, Elizabeth included! She quickly became tired of people making teasing remarks about her being the 'Naughtiest Girl', as they came up and counted the buttons on her blazer!

The following morning she went along to the school gardens. She found John Terry netting the strawberry beds. He was very pleased to see her.

'Hello, Elizabeth. How good to see my best little helper! This job can be done quite quickly now there are two of us.'

Elizabeth was relieved to see that the majority of the strawberry plants remained untouched and were bushing out well, with plenty of green fruit. The uprooted ones from the first row had now been tidied up into a small heap beside the path. They were already withering and well beyond being saved. They were mostly poor, thin things, she noticed, with not many berries on them. So the damage to the strawberry crop had not been as bad as feared, then. How stupid of someone to expect to find some ripe fruit in this way.

'I don't usually net the plants so soon,' explained John, as they unrolled the lengths of fine green netting and placed them carefully over the beds. 'They're to stop the birds getting at the ripe fruit – especially the blackbirds! They take not the slightest interest until they see a strawberry that's red and luscious and at its very peak! If you see a blackbird pecking at one, you can be quite sure that it has just reached its very moment of perfection!'

'How very clever of them!' laughed Elizabeth, her mouth watering as she remembered the days of strawberries and cream at the end of term last summer. 'I wonder how they know? So you've decided to prepare the defences well in advance?'

'Yes,' nodded John.

Once the nets were laid in place, they staked them down by driving small pegs in the ground all the way round the edges. The birds, John explained, would try to wriggle under them if they saw any good gaps.

'Then, as often as not, they can't find their way out again!' he explained. 'They get in such a panic before they manage to escape. Sometimes you find an especially silly one tangled in the netting and you have to release it. However that won't happen for a while yet.'

When they had finished, Elizabeth straightened up and arched her back. It had been hard work. She surveyed the covered beds with a sigh of satisfaction.

'Did you decide to net them early because of what one of the children has done, John?' she asked quietly.

He nodded.

'Yes. If anyone's ever tempted to meddle with the strawberry plants again, it will remind them not to,' he said. 'Silly young idiots. I'm very surprised that nobody's owned up yet. But that blazer button is going to give them away.'

'It certainly is,' agreed Elizabeth. 'And I'm sure they won't dare to do it again!'

When she found Julian, later, she learned that he had been going round with Harry questioning people about blazer buttons.

'We've been getting lots of rude answers, I'm afraid,' he said, with a grin. He yawned. 'This could prove to be quite a long job.'

'The damage isn't quite as bad as John made it sound,' said Elizabeth. 'There should still be plenty of strawberries for tea when it comes to end of term time! Perhaps we should wait a while and see if the person owns up. Oh, Julian, surely they will?'

For by now Elizabeth's mind was turning back to the Summer Play.

On the way back from helping John Terry, she had seen Arabella, with the faithful Rosemary, over by the cedar tree, trying to say some lines off by heart while Rosemary held the script and acted as prompter.

Now that Elizabeth had read *A Woodland*

Adventure through from beginning to end, she longed more than ever to be chosen for the leading girl's role. There were such sparkling lines for Fay to speak, especially in the scenes with Jonkin, the funny goblin who – surely! – could only be played by Julian.

And the two main parts would be auditioned first, on Monday! The joint heads were coming along and would give their opinions to Miss Ranger, although leaving her with the final decision. Later in the week, in other English lessons, the rest of the parts would be given out.

'Julian, we must decide which bits we want to act out on Monday,' said Elizabeth, 'and then we'd better learn the lines off by heart. Will you test me when I've learnt mine?'

'I'll test you tomorrow,' promised Julian, who had arranged to play tennis with Harry for now. 'Mind you learn them well!'

By Sunday evening, Julian had still not bothered to learn any lines of his own and treated the whole thing in his usual casual way.

'Stop fussing, Elizabeth. I haven't decided which bit I want to act out, yet. I'll get something together by tomorrow, I daresay.'

Elizabeth, on the other hand, had learned three different sections of Fay's part, skimping most of her prep that weekend in order to do so.

'I'll act out each bit in turn, Julian, and you tell me which one you think is best.'

Julian watched and listened attentively and gave her some good acting tips, too, as she went along.

'I liked the first one best,' he said, at the end. 'When Fay wakes up in the woods and finds that she's turned into a fairy queen and she thinks she's all alone until Jonkin peeps out from behind the tree! You do it very well. Do you know something? I think you could be a real star!'

He looked really proud of her as he said it.

Elizabeth's mouth went dry with excitement.

She could hardly wait for the auditions to begin.

When Elizabeth arrived for English the next day, she noticed Julian already in his place,

casually flicking through the pages of the script.
So he still hadn't learned any lines! By the look
of him, he was only just starting to think about
it. Elizabeth felt cross. But she knew that she
must concentrate hard now and not let
anything distract her.

'We will start with Fay's part,' the teacher
was saying. 'Belinda, would you like to go first,
please?'

Miss Belle and Miss Best, the joint heads, were
sitting at the front with Miss Ranger. Belinda
stood up and launched into her lines. It was all
very exciting. Elizabeth watched and held her
breath and wondered how well Belinda would
do.

She had chosen a tender scene in the play
where Fay finds the injured Mr Badger in the
woods. She acted it out quite well, though she
did forget her lines once or twice. When she sat
down, everybody clapped her.

'Your turn now, Elizabeth,' smiled Miss
Ranger.

'May I sit on the floor, under the window
here, please?' asked Elizabeth. 'You will all have

to imagine I'm sitting under the big tree, just waking up from a sleep, right at the beginning of the play.'

The joint heads nodded in approval. They were enjoying seeing their play start to come alive. Everybody in the class turned round to watch Elizabeth's performance. Somehow, she riveted the attention.

She began by stretching and yawning and then opening her eyes.

She stared all around her in wonderment.

'*Why am I here? Where have I been?*'

Then she stood up and ran her hands down her clothes.

'*Why am I dressed as a fairy queen?*'

Elizabeth continued her monologue, word perfect, acting it out as she went. She sighed, she gasped, she pirouetted, as she discovered the beautiful woods for the first time. It all seemed so real. She ended by subsiding back down to the floor again, once more under her 'tree', her voice a little sad.

'*. . . but when nightfall comes I'll be all alone.*
And missing my dearest friend from home.'

She gave a big sigh, as the script had directed.

Her performance should have ended at that point. But suddenly Julian stood on his chair, jumped off, hopped lightly over to Elizabeth's desk then ducked behind it. He peered at her round the corner, pretending the desk was a tree. Face screwed up like a goblin's, green eyes sparkling, he launched into Jonkin's part –

'Alone my foot, alone my thumb
Come, my Royal Highness. Come!'

He pulled Elizabeth to her feet and danced her round the desk –

'You'll meet new friends in this wood so green
And all of them love their fairy queen!'

It was so unexpected that Elizabeth laughed in excitement. Her audition really was over now and her classmates were cheering and clapping. The teachers were smiling, too. But then Miss Ranger held up a hand for silence.

'Very good, Julian. But we're not auditioning for Jonkin's part yet. Your turn will come in a few minutes. Thank you, Elizabeth. Now let us see what Arabella can do, please.'

Arabella was the third and final girl asking to

be considered for the part of Fay. She rose to her feet, face pale with tension.

'Please, Miss Ranger, I've learnt the same bit as Elizabeth. The opening bit. And I was planning to sit and lean against the wall, just as she did.'

'That's perfectly all right, Arabella,' said Miss Ranger gently.

The fair-haired girl, looking as pretty as a picture, went and sat on the floor under the window – very much as Elizabeth had done.

Biting her lip in annoyance, Elizabeth had to watch and listen as her rival repeated all her actions. She stretched, she yawned, she opened her eyes . . .

'Why am I here? Where have I been?'

Arabella was striving hard to be expressive. It was a good effort – and there was no doubt that she looked the part.

But then, on her second line, she made a silly mistake.

Carefully imitating Elizabeth's action and smoothing down her clothes she said –

'Why am I queened as a fairy dress?'

Snorts and giggles broke out round the classroom and Miss Ranger had to bang the table for silence. Stumblingly, Arabella corrected herself and carried on through the opening monologue.

In spite of fluffing some more lines, and forgetting one line completely, it was quite an impressive effort. The boys and girls gave Arabella a good round of applause at the end. The teachers joined in. As Arabella returned to her seat, pink with excitement, Elizabeth began to feel very tense.

'We will now audition for the part of Jonkin,' announced Miss Ranger. 'After that I shall have a private chat with Miss Belle and Miss Best and then at the end of the lesson the parts will be given out.'

Elizabeth could hardly bear the suspense.

6 *Elizabeth is over excited*

Several boys wanted to be in the play, especially in the roles of Mr Badger and Mr Grasshopper. They were both such good characters! Those two roles would no doubt be fought over, later in the week. But only two boys wanted to try for the Jonkin part as it looked quite daunting.

The other one was Daniel. He was called first and even he seemed hesitant.

'I – I'm not that sure I want to try for it,' he said, awkwardly. 'Not really.'

'Oh, come along, Daniel,' chided Miss Ranger. 'You know you can do it.'

Elizabeth could see that the fair-haired boy was embarrassed. It was odd, how Daniel had returned to his old ways lately. He had been so different last week, lively and cheerful, even asking Martin to test him for the play! Since then he had become his usual self again. It was true that he was spending a lot of time at the school stables, after speaking to the stableman. But Robert had complained that he was not really helping much. He read his books all the time, or simply lazed around, exactly as before. He might just as well have been in his room! What a funny boy he was, thought Elizabeth.

But now she felt uneasy. She remembered Julian's idea that the teachers had forced Daniel to put his name down for the play. Was it possible there might be favouritism?

Daniel began his first line, still embarrassed.

'Wait, Daniel!' said Miss Ranger, holding her hand up. Smiling gently, she rummaged in a bag. 'Look, this might help you. In the play, Jonkin always wears a mask. A lot of the animal characters will wear masks, too. Let's see you put this mask on, as you act out your lines. You may find that it helps you get into the spirit of things!'

The teacher handed the boy a face mask. It was not the actual goblin mask that would be used in *A Woodland Adventure*. That would not be ready until later. It was just an old mask from the school dressing-up chest but it was a funny one, with an upturned nose and rosy cheeks.

As Daniel put the face mask on, the children laughed and clapped. Elizabeth became even more uneasy. She was sure that Julian was right. The teachers wanted Daniel in the play; they very much wanted him to succeed.

Now, as he acted out the part from behind his mask, the improvement was very marked. He had learned his lines well and his shyness was dropping away. He was much more carefree.

His performance was not too bad at all.

'Congratulations, Daniel,' said Miss Belle, afterwards. 'You did that well. Didn't he, Miss Best?'

The joint heads looked pleased.

'Now, Julian, your turn,' said Miss Ranger. 'And you must wear the face mask, too, so we can judge you both fairly!'

Everybody cheered as Julian put the mask on and went straight into a goblin-like pose, crouching on his chair.

'I'm afraid I haven't learned any lines yet,'

he said, carelessly picking up the script. 'Apart from the little bit I did with Elizabeth. But – let me see – there's a scene here that's rather good, I think.'

Before Elizabeth had time to feel angry with Julian again for being so casual, he had launched forth. It was a passage from the play where Jonkin has decided, secretly, to bake a cake for the fairy queen.

'Here's a pinch of aniseed
I'll find the other things I need
Flower where the sweet bees suckle
And honey from the honeysuckle
Butter from the buttercups . . .'

The class watched and listened in delight. It was hard to remember that Julian was reading from a script, so fluent was his performance. As he spoke the words, he did all the right actions as he went along! He ended up with a handstand, as required by the script.

Everybody clapped. It was a most excellent performance!

'Thank you, Julian,' nodded Miss Ranger, as Julian handed in the face mask. 'You should really have learned your lines, though, like the others.'

Then Miss Ranger told the class to get out their English set books and read them in silence. She wished to confer with the joint heads.

As the three grown-ups went into a huddle, Elizabeth strained her ears, trying to catch what they were saying. But they spoke in very low, soft voices. Soon after that, the joint heads departed from the classroom. *Who had Beauty and the Beast liked best?* she wondered. They, after all, had written the play.

Nevertheless, Miss Ranger was in charge of the first form and was the play's producer. The final decisions on casting must be left to her, for she knew her pupils best.

After seeing Miss Belle and Miss Best out, Miss Ranger came back and stood in front of the class and made her announcement.

'Elizabeth will play the part of Fay,' she said. 'And Arabella will be her understudy . . .'

Elizabeth gave a gasp of pleasure.

'And we will try Julian in the Jonkin part as long as he behaves properly and learns his lines.

Daniel will be the understudy.'

Elizabeth felt weak with happiness as her classmates crowded round and clapped her on the back. 'Well done,' said Belinda, sportingly. 'You were really good.' Julian was being congratulated, too. There was noise and chatter all round.

As the bell went for the end of the lesson Miss Ranger clapped her hands for silence.

'I can see you are all very excited,' she said. 'But remember, please, that this is school time. We have plenty of hard work to get through, if you are all to do well in summer exams at the end of term. The next lesson is geography. I am just slipping out to collect our weather map from Mr Johns . . .'

She looked at them sternly.

'When I return to the classroom, I expect to see you all sitting at your desks in absolute silence, please. You will have your geography books out and be ready to start the next lesson.'

It was rather too much to ask. As soon as the teacher had left, the buzz of chatter broke out afresh. Elizabeth, in particular, was rather over excited.

It had been such a strain, waiting to hear the results of the auditions. Now her dearest wish had been granted. She would play the part of Fay, Julian the part of Jonkin! With Julian cast opposite her, the Summer Play was going to be tremendous fun. She was already looking forward to rehearsals. It was going to be the best thing they had ever done at Whyteleafe School!

She noticed that Daniel was congratulating Julian. He did not seem to resent the fact that he would just be understudy. The same could not be said of Arabella. She was the only person in the class not to congratulate Elizabeth. She was sitting at her desk, head bent, looking out her geography books.

'Cheer up, Arabella,' she called out, boisterously. 'I might fall and break a leg!'

'Yes, you'll make a good understudy, Arabella,' giggled Belinda. 'You copied everything that Elizabeth did to perfection.'

Elizabeth winced. Nothing would have

induced her to raise that herself. But she was touched that some of the others had noticed it.

Arabella looked up, sulkily.

'I did nothing of the sort! I had everything planned already. It wasn't my fault that I had to go last –'

Belinda just laughed and then Arabella lost her temper. She sprang to her feet and pointed at Elizabeth.

'She cheated! She got Julian to help her! I saw them practising together last night. They had it all planned. It's not fair! It was Julian joining in at the end that got her the part!'

'Rubbish!' exclaimed Julian.

Elizabeth felt a temper coming on. She would get her own back on Arabella for saying that. What a mean girl she was!

As Miss Ranger came along the corridor with the map two minutes later, she could hear a commotion in the classroom. What was going on? She stood in the doorway and gazed at the scene.

Elizabeth Allen was standing on her desk,

declaiming loudly, her face flushed with excitement. She was imitating Arabella.

'Why am I here? Where have I been?
Why am I dressed as a hairy fiend?'

Some of her friends had crowded round, hooting and stamping their feet at Elizabeth's impromptu performance.

'SILENCE!' came the voice from the doorway.

The children all scrambled back to their desks. Elizabeth quickly jumped off hers and sat in her place. There was a hurried scuffling of paper and banging of desk lids as they all got their geography things out. Then came complete silence, broken only by muffled snorts as some children struggled hard to stop laughing.

But Miss Ranger's eyes were fixed only on Elizabeth, whose cheeks were still very flushed with excitement.

'I am surprised at you, Elizabeth. Do you not realise that anyone can fluff their lines in a play, even you? Do you not realise that you were being rather cruel and silly?'

Elizabeth opened her mouth to speak. She wanted to tell Miss Ranger how cruel and silly

Arabella had been to her. Not just today, either, but from the very first moment they had met. That dreadful moment in the Christmas holidays when Arabella had come to stay at her house just because their parents knew each other. And Elizabeth's mother had informed her that Arabella was coming to Whyteleafe and would be a nice companion for her, with her beautiful manners and lovely clothes! Why, Elizabeth had hated the spoilt girl on sight.

But, with her mouth still open, Elizabeth remained silent.

'Do you not realise?' repeated the teacher.

'COR!' came the cheeky reply.

It was very loud and sounded deliberately silly and insolent.

There was a moment's shocked silence and then snorts of nervous laughter broke out. That Cor! coming from Elizabeth like that had been such a surprise. And now the Naughtiest Girl was looking all around her, pretending to be surprised herself.

'Who said that?'

'You did, Elizabeth,' replied Miss Ranger. She

did not find it in the least bit funny. 'Stop showing off, Elizabeth. You have just been extremely cheeky to me. You will apologise at once, please.'

'It wasn't me, Miss Ranger!' protested Elizabeth, in bewilderment. She turned and looked out of the open window, which was right behind her. 'It must have been someone fooling around outside!'

She opened the window very wide and leaned out of it, looking right and then left. Several of her classmates rushed from their desks to the back of the room and crowded round her.

'That's funny, there's nobody there,' Elizabeth was saying.

'Ooops! Nobody there!'

'Can you see anybody, Martin?'

'Not a sausage.'

'Must have been a ghost!'

Some of the boys, in particular, were enjoying the distraction. This was the Naughtiest Girl as she used to be! It was good fun and better than geography.

'Sit down, all of you,' exclaimed Miss Ranger.

'Elizabeth, shut that window at once. Now turn round, sit down and face me.'

'Yes, Miss Ranger.'

The teacher spoke in icy tones.

'I see that getting the star part in the play has made you over excited, Elizabeth. You have got completely carried away. If you cannot calm down, I will have to think again about my decision. Now, for the last time, will you please own up and apologise for speaking to me in that rude way.'

The whole class fell silent. The joke was over.

They waited to see what Elizabeth would say.

7 A very bad quarrel

'I have no intention of apologising, Miss Ranger,' said Elizabeth. 'How can I, when it wasn't me?'

The boys and girls looked at the Naughtiest Girl in surprise. Of course it was her! Who else could it have been? They had all heard her. How silly of her to speak to Miss Ranger like that. Now she would lose her part in the play.

Elizabeth did not mean to sound ill-mannered but she had a very hot temper. It was really horrid, not to be believed like this. Even if it meant losing the precious part in the play, she thought angrily, she was not going to pretend she had made that cheeky comment when she had not.

'Really, Elizabeth,' began the teacher, in exasperation. 'You will leave me with no other choice—'

There was a sudden sound.

ZZZZZZZZZZZZ.

It seemed to be coming from Elizabeth's direction, near the window.

ZZZZZZZZZZZ.

There it was again. But this time it was over by the door. Was there a bumble bee flying round the room?

ZZZZZ. ZZZZZZ.

It was buzzing here, there and everywhere. But where was it? Nobody could see it.

Julian! realised Patrick.

And suddenly Julian was grinning and everybody in the class remembered. Julian had done this before! He was absolutely brilliant at imitations. He could throw his voice, too. He could make sounds appear to come from anywhere, without moving his lips . . .

Julian, thought Elizabeth, in horror. *Of course.*

She was not amused.

Nor was Miss Ranger.

'You have been misjudged, Elizabeth,' she said. 'I apologise for that. We had forgotten all about your friend, Julian, hadn't we, and the clever things he can do with his voice? However, I'm afraid there is one clever thing that Julian will *not* be doing with his voice in future. Please stand up, Julian. And take your hands out of your pockets while I am speaking to you.'

She lectured Julian sternly about disrupting the lesson and almost getting Elizabeth into further disgrace.

'I can see that you and Elizabeth are going to be very over excited and silly if you are in the play together,' she concluded. 'I'm afraid I have changed my mind about the part of Jonkin. It will be played by Daniel. You will be Daniel's understudy.'

'Yes, Miss Ranger.'

For the rest of the lesson, the class was very subdued, even Arabella and Daniel.

Elizabeth was subdued, too, but inside she was boiling.

She had briefly felt relief when the mystery was cleared up. She had been completely baffled as to where that voice had come from. She thought it must have come through the window just behind her but, of course, there was nobody there! She never dreamt it had been one of Julian's tricks. It would have been too stupid of him.

But it *had* been him! And if he hadn't let it be known, she could have lost the part in the school play.

Her relief quickly changed to anger, as she thought about his silly behaviour and his own part being taken away from him, which was no more than he deserved. Now she would have to play opposite Daniel, instead. How dull that would be. She had been so looking forward to acting in the play with Julian.

'How could you be so stupid?' she raged at him, after lessons, as soon as they were alone. 'Now Daniel's got your part! You and your silly voices. You've ruined everything!'

Julian's green eyes glittered for a moment.

'If that's what you think, Elizabeth, I don't call you much of a friend.'

'What else am I supposed to think?' exploded Elizabeth. 'Even friendship has its limits!'

'Somebody must have been trying to get you

into trouble and it wasn't me,' replied Julian
coolly. 'I was trying to get you *out* of trouble.'

'Oh, *really*? When nobody else in the class
can throw their voice like that except you,
Julian? Please don't make me any crosser than I
am already!'

Now Julian's own temper snapped.

'In that case, there can be only one
explanation, can't there? I mean to say, it's the
only answer . . .'

'What?'

'Miss Ranger was right all along. You were
completely over excited and you cheeked her
yourself. So over excited you don't even
remember doing it!'

'How dare you!'

Elizabeth turned her back on Julian and
stalked away.

'If that's what you think, I have nothing more
to say to you.'

'Nor I to you,' Julian retorted, as he turned
on his heel and headed in the opposite direction.

It was a very bad quarrel.

In the days that followed, Elizabeth thought

about it many times. But she always reached the same conclusion. Julian *must* have been responsible for that silly voice. There was just no other explanation! He probably realised he had been very foolish indeed. Was it pride that stopped him owning up and saying sorry so that they could be friends again?

But it was mean of him to try to persuade her that *she* had been the silly one, so over excited that she didn't know what she was doing! That would make *her* responsible for his losing his part in the play!

She decided not to speak to Julian again until he apologised.

Julian felt exactly the same way about Elizabeth.

8 *The button's owner is found*

Elizabeth was unhappy for the next few days. It was horrible not being on speaking terms with Julian. She had other friends in the first form but it was with Julian that she got on best. She would like to have seen more of Joan during this troubled time. But with the two girls in different forms that was not possible.

Arabella quickly took advantage of the situation. The vain little girl had no idea why Elizabeth and Julian had mysteriously fallen out but it gave her quiet satisfaction. She was tired of the way everybody liked Elizabeth and nobody liked her.

'We may only be understudies, Julian,' she told him, 'but that still means we have to learn out parts. It's a very important job being an understudy. If anything happens we could easily be called upon.' She gave him a winsome smile. 'I'm an absolute ninny at learning lines. Please help me. We can practise some of the scenes together. I'd love you to test me and I'll be only too pleased to test you.'

One evening, Elizabeth walked into the common room and found them rehearsing some of the play together. Rosemary was their prompter. Arabella was giggling happily.

'Oh, Julian, you are naughty. You're peeping at the script, I can see you. You still haven't bothered to learn it.'

Elizabeth turned on her heel and walked straight out again. It was infuriating. Arabella seemed to be having more fun just being an understudy than she was having in the real play! Julian was allowing her to help him over that blazer button mystery, too. It had still not been solved.

Much of Elizabeth's zest for acting had gone.

The other auditions had taken place and the full cast chosen. Rosemary had been made prompter. Elizabeth was pleased when Belinda, Kathleen and Jenny were all given good supporting roles in the play. John McTavish was picked to play Mr Grasshopper who had some very funny lines to speak. And Patrick, of all people, had landed the part of the poor, sickly Mr Badger. He seemed to be enjoying himself already, all the more so now that Julian had been kicked out of the play.

Elizabeth had vowed to put Julian right out of her mind and throw herself into the play with gusto. After all, Daniel had been rather good as Jonkin, once he wore that funny mask.

But from the very first rehearsal, her spirits sank. It was all Daniel's fault. He had memorized his lines well. He was good at English and had no difficulty with learning by rote. But his acting was so half-hearted! His mind always seemed to be elsewhere. She could strike up no rapport with him. In the scenes they had to act out together, he refused to meet her gaze but just kept glancing shiftily around.

Worst of all, he kept on apologising.

'I'm really sorry you've got me, Elizabeth,' he said, at that very first rehearsal, which took place after school on the terrace. 'I feel terrible that Julian had the part taken away from him.'

'I shouldn't bother to feel terrible about Julian!' retorted Elizabeth, sharply. 'It was no more than he deserved.'

But the boy looked guilt-stricken, all the same, and the apologies kept on coming.

'I'm sorry, that wasn't very good. I'm sure Julian would have done it much better . . .'

By the third rehearsal, Elizabeth was ready to snap.

'If you mention Julian again, I'll scream! Stop being such a drip, Daniel. We've got to make a success of this! I'm begining to think we're going to make complete idiots of ourselves in front of the whole school. Put some verve into it, *please* . . .'

What was the matter with the boy?

It was the weekend and Elizabeth was feeling particularly irritable.

On her way to rehearsal she had noticed Julian, Harry and Arabella talking to some of the juniors. At this week's School Meeting, William and Rita had asked the assembled children to renew their efforts to find out who had vandalised the strawberry plants. Elizabeth would love to have been helping Julian track down that missing blazer button. Instead, he and Harry were allowing Arabella to tag along with them.

In fact, Julian was simply filling in time. Secretly, he was still very hurt and angry at Elizabeth's behaviour – and puzzled, too. As he saw her pass by, he wondered how long it was going to be before she finally came to her senses and apologised to him.

After the rehearsal on the terrace, Elizabeth trudged back into school, her spirits at a low ebb. She was sorry she had lost her temper with Daniel. It was the worst thing she could have said to him! It was silly of her to frighten him like that. At least he had managed not to mention Julian's name again. He had just acted like a frozen rabbit, instead.

'I don't think the play's going to be any fun at all,' Elizabeth concluded. She decided to go upstairs and read a book. She walked towards her dormitory when suddenly she heard her name being called.

'I've been looking for you, Elizabeth.'

Assistant Matron came out of the little sewing room and greeted Elizabeth in the corridor. She carried a small blazer over her arm. Elizabeth recognised the strawberry jam mark on the front! It was hers – one she had outgrown and handed in at the begining of term. She had a much bigger one now which would last longer she hoped.

'I'm checking over all the second-hand uniforms this week, Elizabeth,' smiled Assistant Matron. 'I want to send it all to the cleaners next week. We need everything back in good time for the school uniform sale at the end of term!'

The school second-hand shop did a good trade at the end of the school year, when parents came to collect their children from Whyteleafe. New uniform was so expensive and the children grew so quickly. Some parents were always pleased to have the chance to kit them out in good second-hand items for the new school year ahead.

Elizabeth stared dreamily at her first blazer.

She felt quite fond of it now. She remembered her governess, Miss Scott, taking her to the big store to buy the brand new uniform and, afterwards, reinforcing the blazer buttons with some extra strong blue thread. 'You treat your clothes so roughly, Elizabeth,' Miss Scott had said. 'We don't want the buttons coming off.'

Elizabeth had cheeked Miss Scott at the time, telling her that she would not be at Whyteleafe School long enough for that to happen. She did not *want* to go to a horrid boarding school and would make sure that she was sent home as soon as possible! How silly and childish she had been, thought Elizabeth. She loved her school uniform now. She was very proud to wear it.

Elizabeth realised that Assistant Matron was looking at her expectantly. 'Did you want something, please?' she asked, politely.

'The button, Elizabeth! You promised to give it to me weeks ago.'

Elizabeth's hand flew to her mouth.

In her relief at handing in the uncomfortably small blazer, she had forgotten all about that button! It was the blazer becoming so tight that had made the middle button burst off, in spite of Miss Scott's best efforts. Elizabeth had put the button in a safe place but then promptly forgotten all about it. Now she apologised.

'I'll go and find it straight away. I think I remember where I put it.'

'I have to go to the village now,' said Assistant Matron, smiling. 'Just put it on my sewing table when you've found it, Elizabeth.'

'I will. I promise.'

She hurried into the dormitory and went to her cubicle. A white-painted chest of drawers stood there with pretty blue wooden handles. All the girls had one, next to their beds. On top of her chest of drawers, at the back, was a small china bowl in which Elizabeth kept oddments. A foreign coin, some hair grips, a mouldering bath cube. She was almost certain that she had put the button there for safe keeping, all those weeks ago.

But there was no sign of it now. Elizabeth poked inside the bowl, in puzzlement. Where *had* she put it then? She began to search through the drawers below, turning them out, one by one.

'Lost something, Elizabeth?' asked Kathleen, cheerfully, coming into the dormitory.

At the same moment, Arabella was passing the open door. She paused and peered inside, glancing at Elizabeth. She had just been indulging in a happy day dream. Her faithful friend, Rosemary, had told her what a poor performance Daniel and Elizabeth had put up at today's rehearsal; that Elizabeth had snapped at Daniel and Miss Ranger had not looked very pleased.

Surely it would only be a matter of time before she and Julian would be asked to step into the breach? Instead of being a flop, the Summer Play would be the most brilliant success! In her mind's eye, the sun was shining brightly. She and Julian, hand in hand, were being given a standing ovation . . .

Now, Arabella heard Elizabeth speaking crossly to Kathleen:

'Just a silly old button! I was sure I put it in my little bowl. Assistant Matron needs it! Oh,

Kathleen, do help me look for it. It's a silver blazer button with some bright blue thread hanging from it.'

Arabella nearly gasped out loud.

She quickly tiptoed away down the corridor, feeling surprised and excited. She must tell Rosemary about this and they must think what to do.

Less than half an hour later, Jenny came up to the dormitory.

Elizabeth looked hot and bothered. It seemed to be one of those horrid days when *nothing* would go right. She and Kathleen had ransacked the cubicle. They had even pulled the chest of drawers away from the wall, no easy task, to see if the button could have slipped off the top and down the back. They had looked under Elizabeth's blue rug. They had even crawled under her bed. It was nowhere to be found.

The loss of the button somehow filled Elizabeth with uneasiness, although she could not think why. And now Jenny had appeared in the doorway and was looking at her rather strangely.

'Can you come down to the common room, please, Elizabeth?' she asked, unhappily. 'Something important's cropped up.'

When Elizabeth entered the common room, Arabella was sitting at one of the little tables. A few of their classmates sat nearby, watching with interest. There was a sense of expectancy in the room.

Something was lying on the table. Arabella placed it on the palm of her hand. Then, with a flourish, she held it out towards Elizabeth.

'Was this what you were looking for?'

Elizabeth stepped forward and examined the object closely. It was a silver blazer button with some bright blue thread hanging from it.

'My button!' she exclaimed. 'Where did you find it, Arabella?'

'William and Rita had it,' said Arabella, with a meaningful look. 'Rosemary and I heard you were looking for one. We've just been along to their study and borrowed it from them!'

'It's the button that John found in the strawberry beds!' said Rosemary solemnly. 'We were all asked to find out who owns it, remember? And now we have!'

Elizabeth looked at the button in complete astonishment.

'You surely don't think I was the person trying to steal strawberries?' gasped Elizabeth.

'We all like strawberries,' said Arabella, pursing her lips.

'I haven't worn my old blazer for weeks! Ask Assistant Matron if you don't believe me!' snapped Elizabeth, her temper flaring up. 'I'd never wear it to the school gardens, anyway. I've absolutely no idea how the button got *there*! I put it in the little bowl on top of my chest of drawers, weeks ago, and that was the last time I saw it!'

'Perhaps you just *meant* to do that,' suggested Arabella. 'Perhaps you actually had it in a pocket and it fell out one day when you were messing about in the gardens . . .'

'How dare you!' raged Elizabeth.

Before she could lunge at Arabella, Rosemary stepped between them. She spoke soothingly.

'Now, it's no use getting angry with Arabella, Elizabeth. William and Rita said that if you *did* recognise the button you were please to go and see them in their study at four o'clock. You can explain it all to them in the proper way.'

'Indeed I shall!'

She stormed out of the common room.

9 Julian makes it five

For all her bravado, Elizabeth felt scared as she tapped on the door of William and Rita's study at four o'clock. How had her button got there? It was dreadful to be under suspicion like this. Surely the head-boy and girl knew her too well to believe that she would damage young plants? Surely they must know that although she might be tempted to pick the occasional ripe strawberry, she would never pull young plants out of the ground to look for fruit! It would be such a stupid and ignorant thing to do.

'Come in, Elizabeth.'

Still quaking, she walked into the cosy little study. William and Rita were waiting for her.

There was somebody else in the room with them, seated in the visitor's armchair. It was John Terry.

Elizabeth felt somehow reassured by the sight

of John, as he stood up and offered the chair to her. She sat down. Everybody seemed very calm.

'John's just been telling us how you helped him net all the strawberry beds, after the plants had been vandalised,' said William approvingly. 'But you do recognise the button, then?'

Elizabeth nodded.

'We know you're one of his best little helpers,' stated Rita. 'We thought we should have a chat with John first about this button business.'

'Don't look so worried, Elizabeth,' smiled William. 'None of us thinks for one moment that you pulled up those plants.'

'Oh, thank goodness,' replied Elizabeth.

'But have you any idea how your button could have got there?' asked Rita. 'Is it possible that you lent it to somebody?'

'Definitely not,' said Elizabeth, with a firm shake of the head. 'I mean, who would want to borrow an old blazer button? Besides, I had to keep it safe because I'd promised to give it to Assistant Matron. It was just that I'd forgotten all about it, until she asked me today.' Elizabeth explained about handing in the old blazer without it. 'The missing button should have been in the little bowl on top of my chest of drawers,' she finished.

At that, Rita smiled and shook her head.

'You must be mistaken there, Elizabeth. You really must! Now try to think very carefully. You *forgot* to give it to Assistant Matron. Is it not possible that you *forgot* to put it in a safe place, too? That you were just carrying it around in a pocket?'

'Well . . .' Elizabeth frowned. She was convinced that she had put the button in the bowl. 'I don't think so. But . . .'

'But it *is* possible, isn't it?' chuckled William. He was looking very relieved. 'Well, I think that's the beginning and the end of your involvement. John has told us how often you help in the garden. You must have been weeding the plants one day and the button fell out of your pocket! The whole thing is a complete coincidence and has nothing to do with the fact that, at a later stage, somebody vandalised them.'

'I – I suppose so,' said Elizabeth, reluctantly. She was still frowning. When had she ever worked in that part of the garden?

'You gave us a red herring when you produced that button, John!' chided Rita.

'It was wrong of me to jump to conclusions,' agreed John, with a wry smile. He scratched his head. 'I thought I'd found a grand clue and I'd found nothing of the sort.'

There was a thoughtful expression on his face as he tried to work it out. He had been so sure that the lost button and the damaged plants were closely linked. But if the two things were unconnected . . . why, perhaps he had been on the wrong track altogether. He must start to keep his eyes and ears open . . .

As Elizabeth left to go to tea, she felt pleased that William and Rita and John believed in her. It did make her feel a little better.

However, as she walked into the dining hall, she could feel the tension in the air as many of the children glanced her way. The whispers had spread very quickly. The mystery of the blazer button had been solved! It belonged to the Naughtiest Girl. She had just been hauled up in front of the head-boy and girl!

Her classmates were less chatty than usual. But her best friend Joan kept looking across from the next table and giving little smiles and waves, to show solidarity.

Elizabeth began to get a horrid feeling in the pit of her stomach. How very bad it must look to everybody, her blazer button having been found where the plants had been vandalised! Even worse was the feeling that somebody must have put it there deliberately. The more she thought about it, the more certain she became that she *had* left the button in the bowl and that things could not have happened in the way that William and Rita had suggested.

At the far end of the table, Julian was eating his tea. He was deep in thought, a moody expression on his face.

Elizabeth had lost her own appetite. She had to force herself to eat the tuna salad, usually a favourite. She left her raspberry yoghurt. She could feel a hot pricking sensation behind the eyes and just as soon as they were allowed to get down from table, she fled. She hurried out into the school grounds, her eyes blurred with tears. She was unaware of footsteps following her. She reached the lovely weeping ash tree, where the Summer Play was going to be performed. She crept under its secret canopy of leaves that almost touched the ground. She wanted to hide, like a wounded animal.

She sat down, leant against the tree trunk and buried her face in her hands.

Everything was going wrong!

It had all started with Julian putting on that silly voice! Since then nothing had gone right. And he *still* wouldn't own up and say he was sorry. How she wished that he would. She needed his friendship so badly now.

'Elizabeth?'

Startled, she looked up and saw Julian ducking under the cascading fronds and coming to join her.

'Hello, bad girl. Now, at last, I hope you will believe me!'

He sat down and put an arm round her shoulders to comfort her.

'There's nothing to cry about.'

'There is! There is! William and Rita and John

believe in me and so does Joan. But that's only four people in the whole school. Nobody else knows *what* to think.'

'Only four?' said Julian. 'Don't you mean five?'

'Five?'

'Yes, you forgot to count me. I believe in you.'

She stared at him, in relief. She dried her eyes.

'Do you really? But, Julian, what did you mean just then—'

'Elizabeth, somebody is trying to get you into trouble. I told you that a week ago. Now perhaps – at *last* – you'll believe me!'

Elizabeth gasped as it dawned on her what Julian was saying.

'Listen, Elizabeth. I did *not* put on that silly voice! Somebody else did. And that button could hardly have *walked* on its own to the school gardens. Somebody placed it there. But do you believe me now?' he asked urgently.

'Yes,' replied Elizabeth, in a very small voice. 'Yes. I do.'

Her mind was in a turmoil. She still did not understand who else in the class could be clever enough to throw their voice in that amazing way. But now she was sure that it was not Julian.

I was trying to get you OUT of trouble was what he had claimed at the time. And she had refused to believe him!

If that's what you think I don't call you much of a friend, Elizabeth he had told her angrily.

Now, she turned to him, her cheeks hot with shame.

'You were right about me not being much of a friend, Julian,' she admitted. She felt bitterly angry with herself for misjudging him so. 'You took the blame to save me from losing my part in the play – and ended up losing your own. And that was all the thanks you got from me! Oh, Julian, I don't know how you can ever forgive me. Why have I got such a silly temper? I'm not surprised if you like Arabella better than me. I can be such a horrid person!'

Julian looked at Elizabeth's grief-stricken face. He stood up, then took her hands and pulled her to her feet.

'Up you get, Elizabeth. Stop moping. It doesn't suit you. Not a bad, bold girl like you!

Arabella? You must be joking!' he said cheerfully. He had waited so long for Elizabeth to apologise and now she had. Everything was all right again. 'Come on, let's see if the ponies are free and go for a ride. It will clear our heads and help us to think.'

As they strolled towards the stables, the warm breeze whispering in the grass, Elizabeth felt like a new person.

'It's horrid to think someone's trying to make trouble for me,' she said, as they saddled up the horses. 'But nothing seems so bad now, Julian. Oh, I'm so glad we've made up our quarrel!'

'We'll soon get to the bottom of this peculiar business,' replied Julian confidently.

At that moment, Robert appeared with Daniel.

'As you don't ride, would you like to walk Captain round the meadow, to give him some exercise?' Robert was saying to the fair-haired boy. 'I've got to go and give Patrick some tennis practice now.'

'If you want me to,' replied Daniel, dully.

'What a strange boy he is,' Elizabeth remarked

to Julian, as they set off on horseback. 'Let's take the bridle path, shall we? He still hasn't bothered to learn to ride. All that fuss about wanting to help at the stables. He doesn't seem to enjoy it very much! He doesn't seem to enjoy being in the play much, either! Oh, Julian, we've got to find out who really cheeked Miss Ranger – and then she'll have to admit she was wrong. About us not being sensible if we act in the play together! She'll have to give you your part back!'

'Oh, I'm not worried about that,' shrugged Julian. He had only put his name down to annoy Patrick!

'Well, I'm worried if you're not!' exclaimed Elizabeth. 'It's really hard work, doing it with Daniel.'

'I expect he'll improve,' said Julian.

They had a lovely ride together and talked a lot about the mystery. It was a very puzzling one. Elizabeth hated the idea that someone had a grudge against her. She could not think who it might be.

'The only person with a motive would be Arabella,' she mused. 'She would so love my part in the play. But I'm quite sure it isn't her.'

'So am I,' agreed Julian. 'She could never throw her voice like that. And she was really surprised about the blazer button, I could tell.'

On their return, they rode back through the meadow.

Daniel was sitting by the hedge, reading a book, while Captain grazed peacefully nearby. A bird was sitting on the old horse's back, pecking at Captain's coat.

'You're supposed to be looking after him!' scolded Elizabeth, as they rode past. 'Can't you shoo that crow away?'

'Captain likes it,' mumbled Daniel, without even looking up from his book.

'Isn't he hopeless?' grumbled Elizabeth, as they passed out of earshot. 'Anything rather than put his book down for a minute. How can he possibly say Captain likes it!'

'But he's right!' laughed Julian. 'Horses are really grateful when members of the crow family sit on their backs! I think that one was a rook.'

'Grateful? Whatever for?' exclaimed Elizabeth.

'The birds search through their coats and get rid of little insects and parasites for them, that's what,' replied Julian, still amused at her indignation. 'Elizabeth, I'm beginning to think you've got a down on Daniel. The poor boy can't do anything right.'

Later, as they rubbed down the ponies, Elizabeth said, 'I haven't really got a down on Daniel. He would be nice if he weren't so odd. But he is hopeless in the play, Julian! We've got to make sure you play Jonkin and not him.'

'You've got *your* part, Elizabeth,' replied Julian, contentedly. 'So that's the main thing. You're going to be a star, I tell you!'

But he spoke too soon.

That same night, the bane of Elizabeth's life struck yet again.

10 *Fire! Fire!*

It took Elizabeth a long time to get to sleep. She tossed and turned, listening to the gentle breathing of the other girls in dormitory six. She was so excited about the play and what Julian had said about her being a star. But she was also fearful. Why should someone be trying to get her into trouble? Who could it be?

Soon, it was dusk outside and every other child in the school was fast asleep.

At last she began to feel sleepy.

Her eyes closed.

She started to drift away into a light, fitful sleep ... Then – a sudden raucous cry reverberated in her head –

Fire! Fire!

Was it a bad dream?

Fire! Fire!

There it was again! It seemed to be coming

from outside. Someone was screeching a warning. The school was on fire!

Half asleep and half awake, Elizabeth tumbled out of bed in a panic.

'Wake up everyone! Please wake up! I think the school's on fire!'

She stumbled out into the corridor and rang the fire bell.

CLANG! CLANG! CLANG! CLANG!

The fire bell rang out all over the building.

There was great excitement as sleepy children emerged from dormitories in dressing gowns, rubbing their eyes.

'Fire!' cried Elizabeth. 'There's a fire somewhere in the school!'

They all formed orderly lines, as they had often been drilled to do, then left the building by the special Fire Exits.

Elizabeth led the way.

'Keep calm, everyone!' she cried. 'Make sure everybody's out of your dormitory.'

As they milled around on the lawns outside there was much chattering and ado. Where was the fire? They couldn't see any smoke! But there *must* be a fire somewhere. Elizabeth had rung the fire bell! Oh, thank goodness, it could only be a small one . . .

Now the teachers were appearing. None of them had gone to bed yet. They were still fully dressed.

'There's a fire somewhere, Miss Ranger!' cried Elizabeth. 'I heard someone screaming—'

'Are you sure, Elizabeth?'

While the children waited outside on the chilly lawns, the teachers carried out a full inspection of the school premises.

There was no fire.

Mr Johns returned and spoke to the assembled pupils.

'Back to bed, all of you! A false alarm, I'm pleased to say. Form into lines and go quietly back to your dormitories. There is no sign of a fire anywhere. You are quite safe.'

When Elizabeth reached dormitory six, she found Miss Ranger waiting for her. The expression on the teacher's face gave her a feeling of intense foreboding.

'Go straight back to bed, Elizabeth. That was

a very silly joke. I will see you in the morning, after I have had a chat with Miss Belle and Miss Best.'

The next day, in spite of all her protests, Elizabeth had her part in the school play taken away.

'I am extremely surprised at you, Elizabeth. I accept your word that you did not deliberately set out to play a joke. But your imagination is obviously in a feverish state. From the moment you were given the star part in the Summer Play you have been much too over excited. It is a great shame but I have decided to give Arabella her chance. I am sure she will be more sensible. You will be the understudy.'

Tears came to Elizabeth's eyes. But this time they were tears of pure anger.

She went to find Julian.

'I know jolly well that I didn't imagine those cries. They were real as could be. Oh, Julian, don't you see? Somebody else must have heard them. Not just *me*.'

'Yes, surely,' agreed Julian. 'And somebody

made them, too. Which direction did they come from? Can you remember?'

'I was half asleep . . .'

'Think hard,' coaxed Julian.

Elizabeth frowned in concentration.

'Well, my window was open. It was somewhere outside . . . but sort of *above*. As though there was a fire on the floor above and somebody was leaning out of their window up there and screeching down to me, in a panic.'

'The attic floor, eh?' said Julian calmly. 'Well, we'll question all the children who sleep in dormitory ten, that's the one upstairs, isn't it?'

'Yes,' said Elizabeth eagerly. 'And three or four children have their own little rooms, as well. Oh, surely *someone* up there will have heard something?'

'Lucky it's Sunday. No lessons. It gives us all day to investigate. We're going to get to the bottom of this, Elizabeth, don't you worry,' he said, airily.

It was a great comfort to have Julian by her side that day. Joan, too, was very loyal.

'I am quite sure you will be vindicated,

Elizabeth,' she said, sweetly. 'Somebody else must have heard something, as you say. Is there anything I can do to help? Would you like me to question everybody in the second form?'

'Oh, would you, Joan? That would be such a help. Julian and I are going to quiz everyone who sleeps on the top floor. I *think* the cries came from above. But, of course, I can't be certain.'

Most of Elizabeth's classmates were very impressed by her sincerity, as she went around with Julian talking to people. They were puzzled and bewildered by the whole affair, just as they had been about the blazer button. They hoped, for the Naughtiest Girl's sake, that everything was going to turn out all right for her in the end. It had been rather exciting, hearing the fire bell go off like that! But of course the teachers did not see it that way. And now she had lost her part in the play.

Arabella should have been in a sunny mood that day. But she felt oddly tense and irritable. It was extremely annoying that Julian and Elizabeth, who had mysteriously quarrelled, had now just as mysteriously made it up.

It had been such a triumph when Miss Ranger told her that she, Arabella, was to play the part of Fay in *A Woodland Adventure* and must do her very best to make a success of it. She fully expected some of her classmates to come and find her and congratulate her and wish her luck. But she waited in vain. They all seemed more interested in Elizabeth's predicament and the detective work that she was doing with Julian. As the day wore on, Kathleen and Harry joined in, too, trying to help Elizabeth.

'Did you hear anyone shout "Fire!", Arabella?' asked Kathleen.

'Of course I didn't!' replied Arabella scornfully. 'Elizabeth just made it up.'

'What a waste of time!' agreed Rosemary.

'We're having a play rehearsal soon,' said Arabella. 'Are you coming to support me? I'm a little bit nervous because Rosemary says Daniel's the most terrible actor. You won't find anybody who heard any shouts in the night because nobody did.'

On that point, at least, Arabella was correct.

One by one, Elizabeth and Julian tracked down all the children who slept on the top floor. It was a long task. They were all out and about, enjoying their various weekend activities. And it was a fruitless task, too. For, one by one, the children shook their heads when questioned.

'Think *very* hard, James,' urged Julian. His room, like Daniel's, was almost directly above Elizabeth's window. 'Did you hear someone cry out? In their sleep, perhaps? Someone having a bad dream about a fire?'

'I was dead to the world,' said James. 'I didn't hear a thing – except the fire bell. And I didn't even hear that at first.'

It was the same old story.

'Why don't you try Daniel?' he suggested. 'I often hear him moving around after Lights Out. I think he reads in bed.'

After that, Elizabeth and Julian went to look for Daniel. He was their last hope. But they had not seen him all day.

'I expect he's reading a book in the stables,' commented Julian. 'That's where he usually is these days.'

'Or else *under the haystack fast asleep*, like Little Boy Blue!' said Elizabeth, witheringly.

He was nowhere to be found.

'Surely he can't be spending all day in his room?' suggested Elizabeth, suddenly. 'He used to sometimes. Even lovely sunny days like today.'

Sure enough, they found Daniel in the small bedroom under the eaves. He was not even reading. He was lying on the bed, staring up at the skylight. His play script lay on the bedroom floor.

'Daniel!' exclaimed Elizabeth. 'You lazy lump!'

The boy sat bolt upright with a guilty start.

'I – I'm just learning my lines,' he said, feebly. He picked the script up off the floor and pretended to flick through it. 'What do you want?'

There seemed to be a strange pallor about his face.

'I didn't hear anything, no!' he burst out, as Julian questioned him. He seemed rattled and upset. 'I was fast asleep. Cross my heart and swear to die.'

Julian's interest quickened. He was sure that Daniel was speaking the truth. So why was he looking so upset?

'But you have an idea who it might have been, then?' he asked, probingly.

'It – it could have been . . .' he began to blurt out.

'Yes?' asked Elizabeth, eagerly.

The boy clammed up.

'I don't know,' he said worriedly. 'It could have been anything, I suppose.'

At that moment Rosemary burst into the room.

'So there you are, Daniel! Miss Ranger sent me to find you. You're supposed to be at play rehearsal!'

'Do I have to be?' he asked miserably. 'Can't Julian have a turn? I don't feel like it today.'

'Don't be silly!' said Rosemary. She grabbed him by the arm. 'You're keeping everybody waiting.'

As she hustled him out of the room, Julian and Elizabeth followed them downstairs. Julian was humming to himself, cheerfully.

'I think we're getting somewhere at last,' he said. 'I think Daniel knows something.'

'Yes,' agreed Elizabeth. 'So do I.'

Again she found it difficult to get to sleep that night. The dramatic events of the weekend were spinning round in her head. But now she was beginning to feel a glimmer of hope.

Arabella and Daniel were never going to last out in the play! She had heard from Kathleen that today's rehearsal had been a shambles!

Daniel's confidence had suddenly gone completely. And Arabella could not be of any help to him. She was a bag of nerves herself. She kept fluffing her lines. She had come back from the rehearsal with her face like a thundercloud. It was gradually dawning on her how much she was taking on and that failure stared her in the face.

Meanwhile, thought Elizabeth, she and Julian were getting to grips with the mystery. They had tried to pump Daniel again this evening, without success. But it was perfectly obvious that he suspected who the culprit was. He was shielding somebody! They would have to be patient but surely they would discover the truth soon? Then she and Julian would be able to clear their names. Their parts in the play would be given back to them!

Elizabeth was just drifting off to sleep when there came a sudden thump at the door. She sat bolt upright in bed. There was another thump, followed by a tapping sound . . .

This time she was wide awake!

Fire! Fire! came the choking cry. It was coming from the corridor. What an eerie sound!

'They're trying to trick me again!' she gasped. 'They're in the building this time. They're hoping I'll ring the fire bell again!'

Trembling, she slipped out of bed. She donned her dressing gown and tiptoed towards the door. *Tap . . . tap . . . tap.* There was that noise again. She was frightened. But of one thing she was certain:

I'm not going to be caught out a second time! I know perfectly well there isn't a fire! she decided. *I've got to catch them, whoever it is!*

11 The naughtiest girl
saves the day

As Elizabeth edged open the door she heard rapid movements outside. She peered into the dimly-lit corridor. There was nobody there. They had moved along the corridor and disappeared round the corner. She could hear little bumps and thuds coming from the direction of the attic staircase.

She raced along in pursuit, turned the corner and bounded up the first few stairs in the gloom.

Suddenly with a whoosh and a flutter, a black shape hurled itself at her legs and tried to peck at them.

Krrraaaa! Krrraaaa! Fire! Fire! it seemed to cry.

'A crow!' she gasped. 'A big black crow! How did it get indoors? Whatever's the matter with it?'

It was one of the most startling moments of Elizabeth's life. The bird was extremely agitated. It was still trying to peck at her legs.

Krrraaaa! Fire!

It was uncanny how human it sounded.

After that first shock, Elizabeth felt a sudden rush of relief. Her 'enemy' of the previous night had been no more than a silly black crow! A crow whose cries sounded almost like human ones. It must have alighted very briefly on her window sill last night. Right by her open window. No wonder none of the sleeping children had heard the noise.

'I must get the teachers, quickly!' decided Elizabeth. 'They'll help get the bird out of the building. And now they'll see that I was *not* imagining things!'

As she tried to leave, the crow flew at her legs again.

'Do stop it—!' began Elizabeth, crossly.

Then she stopped.

A tiny wisp of smoke came curling down the attic staircase. Then another. And another.

She caught a faint, acrid smell . . .

'There *is* a fire up there!' she realised, in horror. 'There really is a fire!'

She went hurtling up the long staircase to the very top. The bird was fluttering and flapping around her head the whole time, in full cry. *Kraa! Kraa! Kraa! Kraaa!*

'The smoke's coming from Daniel's room!' she realised.

His door was only slightly ajar but, even from here, the smell was now becoming overpowering. It was the most horrid smell, like burning chemicals . . .

She pushed open the door and then reeled back. There were no flames but the room was full of suffocating smoke. The fair-haired boy lay prone on his bed, overcome by the fumes.

Daniel's passed out! she thought. *I've got to get him out of there, quickly.*

But the acrid smoke was already filling her mouth and nostrils. She felt as though she would pass out, too. She closed Daniel's door for a moment and dived into the bathroom next door. She held a towel under the cold water tap until it was soaking wet.

Then, with the wet towel wrapped firmly round her face, she returned to the smoke-filled room and pulled Daniel to the floor. Her eyes were not covered by the towel and were already smarting painfully. She tried to ignore the pain.

Above their heads, the panic-stricken bird wheeled out of the open skylight. It flew high into the sky and away into the distance. The skylight – *so that was how it had got in!* realised Elizabeth.

'Get flat on your tummy, Daniel!' She gasped. 'So we're down below the level of the fumes . . .'

But the boy was still unconscious.

Slithering slowly backwards towards the door, Elizabeth dragged him, inch by inch, across the polished wooden floor. It took less than a minute but that minute seemed like an hour. Several times Elizabeth started to choke. She was having to keep her eyes tightly shut now. She became scared that she, too, might lose consciousness before she could get Daniel to the door.

Then, at last, they were safely outside.

She slammed the door shut on the smoke-filled room. She knew that it would help to contain the fire. She rubbed the wet towel over her smarting eyes and then over Daniel's face, trying to revive him.

'Daniel. Daniel. Are you all right?'

His face twitched.

'Where am I? What's happened?'

'You passed out!' whispered Elizabeth, through her coughs. 'There's some horrible kind of fire in your room. This bird came and told me about it. A black crow—'

Daniel's eyes opened wide.

'You mean Rookie? He came and fetched you? Then, it *was* Rookie last time. I wondered if it could have been. And tonight there really *was* a fire—?'

'Rookie?' asked Elizabeth, in surprise. Daniel seemed to know all about the bird! 'Why do you call him that?'

'He's my pet. He's my tame rook. He's the brightest, best little rascal that ever lived.'

Daniel gulped.

'But I'm so ashamed, Elizabeth. He's brought you and Julian nothing but trouble. And now I can't keep him secret any more, the teachers will send him away. He'll have to go, won't he?'

'I've got a funny feeling inside me that he's gone already,' whispered Elizabeth.

Suddenly she heard voices below and clattering footsteps.

The teachers had seen the plume of smoke coming out of Daniel's skylight. Now, armed with fire extinguishers, they came running up the stairs.

'What's happened? Are you all right, Daniel?' asked Mr Warlow.

'We'll soon put the flames out!' exclaimed Mr Johns, extinguisher at the ready.

'Please, Mr Johns, there aren't any flames yet,' warned Elizabeth, 'just these horrible poisonous fumes. You'll need wet towels round your faces!'

It was good advice. The two teachers were grateful for it as they charged into the room and squirted a smouldering toy on the bedside locker, then swiftly retreated. There was no risk of a fire spreading now. They had found the cause of all the smoke.

It was against school rules to have foam-filled toys but Daniel had brought a teddy mascot from home without knowing it was stuffed with the forbidden material.

It was also against school rules to read after Lights Out. It was even more strictly forbidden to read by candlelight. Daniel had been doing both. Nor had he remembered to blow the candle out. As he slept, the lighted candle had overbalanced. It had fallen against the teddy bear which had smouldered away, releasing the clouds of acrid fumes into the little bedroom.

'You won't be sleeping in there tonight, Daniel,' Mr Johns told the boy. 'It will take some hours for the room to air.'

Matron decided that both Daniel and Elizabeth should sleep in the sanatorium that night. She wanted to keep a watchful eye on them.

'Daniel has been very silly and Elizabeth has been very brave,' she stated. 'But they have both had a nasty shock. What they both need now is some medicine and a good night's sleep.'

By the following morning both children were fit and well again.

And James, who had been rudely awakened

by the commotion on the attic landing, was soon spreading the dramatic news all round the school.

Elizabeth had heard those cries again! Why, he had half heard them himself. They had woken him up. And this time there really *had* been a fire. It was in Daniel Carter's room. Daniel had passed out in the smoke and fumes. He might have *died*!

Elizabeth had dragged him to safety.

The Naughtiest Girl had saved the day!

'You must have had a premonition on Saturday night Elizabeth,' whispered Kathleen, in awe, when Elizabeth appeared for French. 'Isn't it weird?'

'Please do not talk in my lesson, Kathleen!' exclaimed Mam'zelle '*Silence, s'il vous plait.*'

Elizabeth and Julian exchanged secret smiles.

Over a delicious breakfast that Matron had cooked for them that morning, Daniel had told Elizabeth everything. After that, she had wasted no time in finding Julian. He had been so quick to spot that Daniel was trying to shield someone. Now she was able to tell him who it was!

Very soon, the whole school would hear about it, too.

12 William and Rita have a story to tell

It was very unusual for a School Meeting to be called in the dinner hour. But then this was going to be a very unusual Meeting.

'We may have to decide upon a punishment for somebody,' William told the rows of assembled pupils. 'But first we have a story to tell you.'

'Once upon a time,' began Rita, 'there was a boy who was not very happy at his boarding school. He liked to read a lot and he liked to have privacy. In fact, his mother and father requested he be given a little room to himself. As things turned out that, perhaps, was not such a good idea ...'

The audience listened, fascinated, as the head-boy took up the thread of the story.

'He liked going home for the holidays and

these Easter holidays were especially enjoyable. You see, on the first day of the holidays, he found a baby bird that had fallen from its nest. He took it indoors and nursed it back to health. It was a baby rook, so he called it Rookie. He hand-reared it. First of all he fed it with bread and milk. Soon it needed a richer diet and he went out every day and dug up worms for it to eat. It grew very fast indeed . . . Your turn now, Rita.'

The head-girl smiled at the spellbound children.

At the very back of the hall Miss Belle, Miss Best and Mr Johns sat listening quietly. They had given their permission for Daniel's story to be told.

'Members of the crow family cannot really be tamed. Rookie was no exception. He was soon into everything, jumping into the butter in the kitchen, pecking at the soap in the bathroom. Outside, he would dive-bomb the bonfire in the garden, trying to attack the smoke! The family would cry *Fire!* to warn him. Unlike the magpie, or the jay, or the hooded crow, the rook can make a *great* variety of sounds if it wants to, not just the usual cawing,' explained Rita. She smiled again. 'Soon Rookie could scream *Fire!* himself. But he still kept attacking the bonfire smoke, in the same foolish way!'

'He was finally cured of the habit,' interrupted William, 'when he flew too close to the flames one day and almost singed his feathers. He had a healthy respect for smoke after that! By this time, his young owner was back at boarding school for the summer term.'

'While the boy was away at school he often thought about Rookie,' continued Rita. 'He did love his wicked pet so. He missed him. He could hardly wait for half term. When he got home, he found that Rookie was now full-grown and was becoming very boisterous. In fact, unmanageable. He would wait for the postman in the front garden and try to peck at his legs! And, that very half term week, something dreadful happened. Rookie took a liking to the young strawberry plants growing in the next door garden. He kept pulling them out of the ground. The next door neighbour would have been pleased to shoot him!'

Some of the pupils gasped. The story was getting very exciting. Strawberry plants! A bird with a warning scream! Now they were certain that they knew what this was all about.

'What happened next?' cried some of the juniors.

'What happened next,' said William, gravely, 'was that the boy's parents realised that they could cope with Rookie no longer. At the end of the boy's half term holiday, before they took him back to school, they told their son that he must say goodbye to Rookie. For good. Very soon now, they would release the bird somewhere in the countryside, back into the wild.

'So for the first day back at school, the boy was very sad, as you can imagine . . . Until, by the stables the following afternoon, a bird flew down from a treetop nearby and settled on the boy's shoulder. It was Rookie! The bird had followed the car back to school. It had secretly taken up residence at his young master's school!'

It was Rita who brought the story to its conclusion.

'The boy was overjoyed. The bird loved him! It had refused to be parted from him! He plucked up his courage. At the first School Meeting he fully intended to beg for permission to keep Rookie at school. He was just about to put his request to that fateful Meeting. When . . .'

Rita looked round the hall.

'What happened?'

The juniors called out the answers.

'You said about the strawberry plants!'

'Daniel knew it must be Rookie!'

'He was scared Rookie would be sent away. So he made it up about helping in the stables, instead!'

'He knew Rookie was living down there and he wanted to be with him sometimes.'

The head-girl nodded.

'The bird must have flown in through Elizabeth's window one day and stolen her button,' Rita explained. 'And then he saw the strawberry plants to play with instead.'

'So he dropped it!' concluded William.

A buzz of conversation rippled through the hall.

Sitting near the back, John Terry scratched his head and smiled to himself. He had been so sure that the button had been linked to the crime – and he was right, after all! When it had looked as though there was *not* a link, he had begun to wonder if a large bird or even an animal could have been responsible. He had been watching out for signs ever since but had seen nothing. So he had been on the right track both times – but had failed to make the vital connection!

As the noise level in the hall began to rise, William rapped his little hammer sharply on the table.

'Silence, please. Everyone be quiet now. You have all guessed who the story is about. And now Daniel himself wants to stand up and speak to us.'

Elizabeth saw the fair-haired boy nervously clench and unclench his fists. He rose slowly to his feet. Then he took a deep breath. He spoke timidly.

'I want to tell everybody I'm sorry for the bad

things I've done. I know we're not allowed to have matches or candles and I could easily have set the school on fire. I'm very ashamed about that. I'm also *very* ashamed . . .'

He gulped and glanced at Elizabeth. His voice seemed to be drying up in his throat. She gave him an encouraging nod. *Go on, Daniel.*

'. . . that I was so deceitful. I wanted to have Rookie at school with me so badly that I kept quiet and let other people suffer. I *guessed* it was Rookie who made a noise outside our classroom window. I expect he was looking for me. It was one of his cheeky sort-of-human sounds. But I let Julian take the blame! And Elizabeth getting into trouble for ringing the fire bell was even worse! I couldn't be sure, but I guessed she must have heard Rookie. And I didn't own up. I was so miserable about it. I just sat in my room all day. And the worst thing of all has been play rehearsals! How could I enjoy being in the play when I had made other people lose their parts?'

He sat down hurriedly and buried his face in his hands.

William then asked Elizabeth and Julian to stand up.

'You two have had the worst of Daniel's behaviour,' he said. 'Especially Elizabeth. Can you, Elizabeth, suggest to the Meeting what *you* think his punishment should be?'

There was an expectant hush in the hall, as Elizabeth opened her mouth to speak. School waited to hear what she would say.

13 The Summer Play –
and after

Elizabeth had already consulted Julian. The two friends had discussed things very carefully just before the Meeting.

At the end of morning lessons, they had gone with Daniel to the school stables to help him look for Rookie. But the glossy black bird with the white blaze above its beak was not there. It was so sad to see Daniel, walking around and looking up at the trees, calling out 'Rookie?' over and over again.

'You were right, Elizabeth,' he had said, tearfully. 'He *has* gone. And I don't think he'll be coming back.'

Julian had put an arm round the boy's shoulders as the trio walked slowly back to school for dinner.

'It's hard for you to accept, Daniel. But it

will be good if he never comes back. Rooks are not meant to live on their own. No wonder he was so anti-social! They like to live with other rooks, in colonies. It will mean he's been accepted back into the wild.'

Now Elizabeth spoke up at the Meeting.

'Daniel *should* be punished for the fire in his room last night,' she said. 'But he already *has* been. The worst punishment of all. His bird was terrified. The fire and all the commotion frightened Rookie away! He's gone, you see. Daniel's been punished for everything else, too. He's not had a moment's peace since Julian and I lost our parts in the play. His own guilty conscience saw to that!'

She sat down, out of breath.

There was a moment's silence.

Then suddenly everybody was clapping Elizabeth's little speech. It was very fair of her. She had said exactly the right thing.

The head-boy and girl both nodded in approval. So did the monitors on the platform. Joan felt very proud of Elizabeth.

William held up a hand for silence

again. He fixed Daniel with a calm, kindly gaze.

'Love of books is a wonderful thing, Daniel. Favourite storybooks are like dear friends. But they must never be a substitute for caring for *real* people, too. Lost in your storybook last night, burning that candle, you gave no thought to all the real boys and girls here at Whyteleafe and the possible danger of fire.'

Daniel hung his head.

'And caring for birds and animals. That, too, is a grand thing,' William ended. 'But neither should that ever be a substitute for caring for people. In your desire to keep Rookie, you allowed *people* to suffer. You caused Elizabeth, in particular, a lot of pain and unhappiness.'

'Please, William, I know you are right but it was just so amazing that Rookie liked me so much!' blurted out Daniel. 'The way he followed the car, all the way from our village, just so he could stay with me! You see,' he shook his head, 'the trouble with "real people" is that they don't seem to like *me* very much.'

Elizabeth leapt to her feet indignantly.

'That's not true, William. Julian and I like Daniel. We really do!'

She sat down embarrassed.

Then, languidly, Julian got to his feet.

'There's something else that needs clearing up,' he said, casually. 'About *my* having suffered over the play. That's not quite true. The part of Jonkin is such a long one. Surely I can't be expected to start learning it now? I would much rather Daniel kept it.'

'Only Miss Ranger can decide that, Julian,' replied Rita, pleasantly. 'She is the play's producer. Miss Belle and Miss Best will have a say, too. After all, it's their play.'

But the joint heads – and Mr Johns – were already nodding their approval. It was what the teachers had wanted all along for Daniel. They were worried that he never mixed. Julian's surmise had been correct. Furthermore, Daniel should never have been allowed a single room in the first place, the joint heads decided. They would have to rectify the matter.

It was a disappointment to Elizabeth. Julian was

not to be her co-star in the Summer Play, after all. Arabella was left with that consolation, at least.

But Daniel's performance just got better and better.

Although he was still pining for the bird, the boy started to throw himself into rehearsals. It was fun that John McTavish was in the play, as Mr Grasshopper. Since moving in right next to John, in the big dormitory, the two had become good friends.

Julian was in the same dormitory and gave Daniel a lot of coaching. There was no doubt that helped, too.

Most of all, Daniel did not want to let Elizabeth down.

She soon began to get over her disappointment.

The great occasion itself took place on a beautiful midsummer's evening. *A Woodland Adventure* was enacted in the prettiest corner of the school grounds. The weeping ash tree with its trailing fronds made a perfect stage set for Jonkin and the Fairy Queen. Everyone loved the be-masked 'woodland animals' that appeared, disappeared and re-appeared amongst the greenery.

The whole school sat transfixed, not least Miss Belle and Miss Best. They had worked so hard writing a new Summer Play in time for the first form's turn this year. And how well they were doing it! What a success for their play.

Elizabeth was the star of the show. She had to make several curtain calls. But Daniel, too, had some curtain calls for a fine performance.

Beauty and the Beast were delighted with both of them.

Elizabeth lingered in the grounds long afterwards. She wanted this evening to last for ever.

So did Daniel. He was standing by the big sundial at the top of the lawn. Suddenly he looked up into the sky.

'Hello, Dan. What are you looking at?'

He pointed. A cloud of rooks was flying overhead but one of the birds had dropped back. It circled above their heads for a moment.

They both held their breath and waited.

Then, dipping one wing towards them, as if to say goodbye, it flapped away and caught up with its companions.

Elizabeth and Daniel continued to watch as the cloud of birds headed for the distant horizon. Soon, the little cloud became no more than a moving speck against the lowering red sun. Then the birds were gone, and there was only the sun.

About the Author

Anne Digby was born in Kingston upon Thames and is married with one son and three daughters. As a child she loved reading and the first full length book she ever read on her own (and her first introduction to Enid Blyton) was the Blyton translation of Jean de Brunoff's *The Story of Babar, the Little Elephant*, from the French. From there it was a short step to enjoying Enid Blyton's own adventure stories of which her favourite was *The Secret Mountain*. Anne has now had over thity children's novels published of her own, including the *Trebizon* school series and the *Me, Jill Robinson* series of family adventures and has been translated into many languages. This is her third book in the *Enid Blyton's Naughtiest Girl* series.

Another Hodder Children's book

If you enjoyed this Naughtiest Girl
story, look out for the further
adventures of Enid Blyton's Naughtiest
Girl by Anne Digby!

**THE NAUGHTIEST GIRL
KEEPS A SECRET**

Anne Digby

How *can* the naughtiest girl be good at
camp with horrible Arabella in the very
same tent? *Especially* when she's busy
stirring up trouble for Elizabeth's greatest
friend, Joan . . .

Another Hodder Children's book

If you enjoyed this Naughtiest Girl story, look out for the further adventures of Enid Blyton's Naughtiest Girl by Anne Digby!

**WELL DONE,
THE NAUGHTIEST GIRL**

Anne Digby

The worst girl in the school – or the best? It's the end of the school year and Elizabeth's fate will soon be decided!